Rabbit Food Weekend

Nadia Owens

CONTENTS

ACKNOWLEDGMENTS

I give all my praise to God. Thanks be to Him. I am blessed and grateful for this passion of creativity. To my family, thank you for the love and support you all have given me. You all inspire me to be my very best. Thank you for believing in me. To you, dear reader, never give up on your dreams. The world is waiting for you and your bright ideas.
How will you change the world?

Peace.

I prayed, "You remind me of a song that talks about a reckless love. How you left the ninety-nine to go out and save the one. You remind me of a prayer that I say when I need you there. It could be, "Jesus" or "I need you now" and you would appear out of thin air. You could have left me to drown. You could have left me to burn. You could have left me alone. You could have left me in debt. You could have left me with death but you didn't do that. You came back to save me from myself."

The tears began to trickle down my face one by one as I ended my talk with God. They slid off my face and onto the closed Bible in my lap. I had intentions of opening it up to some scripture that would give me peace. Instead, I sat there in that pew

of the Blessed MacKillop Catholic Church lamenting

to God once again. Hoping this time, God would

actually hear me. I was in a tough spot financially.

My finances were losing their grip on me. I only had

so much money left to depend on for me and my son.

I had thought about deciding to go back to working

for my son's father at his company. This weighed

heavily on my heart. I had originally quit working

there about two years ago. I had grown tired of him

and his ungodly ways. But am I the ungodly one to go

back to the ink-written past?

I thought I had enough money saved up that

would keep us afloat until I found a better job.

Unfortunately, no one wanted to hire a former

entertainer. I had become my mother. I've been

coming to Blessed MacKillop over the last 2 years trying to reconcile with God. Maybe He will put me on the right path. Then, the church bells began to sing the chorus of the 3 o'clock hour. I needed to go get Sebastian from school. I wiped the remaining tears away from my face and put the Bible back in the empty slot on the back of the pew in front of me. I, then, looked up at the enormous stained glass window of Jesus in front of me. The eye contact between me and Glass Jesus lasted for at least 45 seconds. I felt like Jesus was staring inside of my soul judging me for the poor choices I've made in life. Maybe it was just my mind playing tricks on me. Jesus would never judge me for my poor choices…or would he? I shook my head back into reality and stood up in the pew. I turned around to make sure I had grabbed my purse, phone, and car keys. I stepped out of the pew, genuflected in front of the altar, and walked out of the church. The main aisle of the church was so long, I felt like I was marching straight into the world's end. The statues of the angels, Mary and Joseph all mocking me as I left the church. I bet they talked about me when I was gone. "Don't make a fool's mistake" or "find another way to provide" is probably what they would say if statues could speak. They aren't living like me in this modern world.

Out the large, wooden doors and down the steps, I made it to my car. My old, 2006 brown Cadillac had seen its days but it still drove like tomorrow was promised. Once in the car, I popped in a Marlboro cig and lit it. I inhaled its dark substance into my lungs and blew out the smoke into the air. I cut on the engine and drove straight down 4 blocks to get my son from school. The cigarette hung from my mouth like it was an ornament. My stomach was still in knots from my church visit but I acted like it wasn't there. After hitting every red light on these blocks, I finally made it to the Evan K. Elementary School. I drove into the school's lot and pulled my vehicle up behind a line of parked cars. Teachers would come to the car and ask which child you're picking up. So, I parked my car, rolled down my windows, and took another hit from my cig. Out of my mouth came a thick cloud that found its way to evaporation. I took 2 more hits of my cig, then felt something lean onto my car. I turned to my right and goddammit! There was an old, busted-up bag leaning on the passenger's side of my car - Miss Irene; one of the science teachers.

"Picking up my son, Bash," I said to Miss Irene.

"Well, hello to you as well, Lennie." Miss Irene said while she looked me up and down. She leaned off of the car and pulled out her radio.

"Sebastian Miles for pickup." Miss Irene said. Miss Irene had never liked me since she learned of my former and soon-to-be current profession. Plus, one night when I came back to get a notebook for Bash, I caught Miss Irene and a janitor having an intimate moment. As I was about to take another hit from my cig, Miss Irene leaned back down onto my car.

"Can I help you, Miss Irene?" I snorted.

"On my way over here, I couldn't help but notice that there was smoke coming from your car. I thought your engine was burning or you were cooking barbeque."

Miss Irene said, followed by a weird witch's cackle. I gave a fake laugh in return to her.

"Do you smell barbeque, Miss Irene, because I sure don't," I asked without batting an eye. Miss Irene leaned back from the car and looked puzzled.

"Lennie, let's not pretend we are blind to what I'm getting at here."

"I know and I ask again, do you smell barbeque?" She sighed and put her wrinkly hands on her hips, "No, I do not smell barbeque." she huffed.

"Neither do I, Miss Irene. You have yourself a blessed one now, you hear?" I said and went back to my Marlboro. Miss Irene once again leaned back onto my Cadillac.

"Do you have to smoke here of all places?" she asked, sternly. I responded,

"Does your husband know the real reason why you

decide to stay late after school most nights? I don't

think "grading papers" is a valid reason to tell him.

Plus, why does the janitor have to help you grade

some papers? Hmm, Miss Irene?". Miss Irene backed

away from the car with the dirtiest look on her face.

"You have a great weekend, Lennie". She said

and walked away from my car.

"Uh-huh, you do the same, Miss Irene. God bless

you!" I hollered from my window, then followed it

with a laugh. Besides, I always put out the cigarette

before Bash gets in the car.

A few minutes went by and I began to see kids

run out of the elementary school. Kids piled inside of

cars and were led across the crosswalk to the

neighborhood adjacent to Evan K. As the kids were

all situated, the line of cars began to move up. So, out goes the Marlboro and parked turned into the drive. I moved my busted buggy up in the line. I pulled up to where my car lined up with the main doors of the school. As I waited for my son to come to the car, I started banging my hands on the steering wheel to the tune of 'We Will Rock You'. I thought I was doing pretty good until I heard the voice of an angel call my name.

"Hi Mom!" my son called out to me.
"Hey there, lambchop!" I called back out to him. I unlocked the door for him as he approached the car. He hopped in the front seat, closed the door, and fastened his seatbelt. Bash leaned over and gave me a big kiss on my right cheek. I kissed him back on his left cheek and messed with his hair. He laughed - just

like his old man. I put the car in drive and we drove

off back to our home.

	"Did you have a good day at school, Bash?" I

asked him.

"Sure did. Although, my math teacher said that we'll

be working on fractions next week. I'm not sure if I

am ready to handle that yet." He said, quietly.

	"Oh, don't worry about it. I know you'll do

your best when the time comes. You're probably the

smartest fifth grader in there."

	"Thanks, Mom. You're always so supportive

of me."

"I'll always be supportive of you, baby bear," I said,

smiling. He cracked a smile and leaned his head onto

my shoulder.

The rest of the ride was full of stories of what Sebastian did at school today. Fifth graders, nowadays, are some creative creatures. We made it back to our home in the Applewood Apartment Complex. There was an open parking spot available right in front of our section. I pulled in and parked the car. Bash and I got out of the car and headed up the steps to our apartment. Our place was nothing fancy. We had one bathroom, one bedroom, a small kitchen that connected to the living room, and a decent-sized closet where the washer and dryer were roommates. The bedroom belonged to Sebastian because I felt like he should have his own space. I slept on the couch in the living room. My neighbor in the apartment next door to us was kind enough to let me store my belongings in her spare closet. Once inside our tiny home, Bash ran to his room to take off his school clothes and I dropped my things on the couch. I, then, made my way to the kitchen to see what I could make for dinner tonight. Every cabinet door I opened contained either dust bunnies, crackers, ramen noodles, or peanut butter that I'm pretty sure was expired.

"Trying to figure out dinner, huh?" Bash's voice spoke from behind me. I turned around in shock because I did not hear him come out of his room. I straightened out my face like nothing was wrong.

"Yea. I need to run to the store to grab some more food. Otherwise, we'll be eating like rabbits this weekend." I chuckled nervously hoping to break the weird setting. Sebastian just stood there with a cute smile on his face. I felt like a bad parent at that moment.

"It's okay, Mom, I can make some ants on a log for dinner tonight."

"We don't have any ants for your log, love," I said to him quietly.

"Oh okay, then I will just eat a log tonight." he giggled and I giggled nervously back to him.

"I will be in my room playing the game with Bugg and Preston if you need me," Bash said, then came over to hug me. I hugged him so tightly that I didn't want to let go of him. I hugged him like it was going to be my last time hugging him; my Sebastian Henry Miles. I kissed him on the top of his dirty, brown hair and released him. He gave a smile and then headed back to his room. Once I heard his bedroom door close, I ran over to the couch and grabbed my purse. I pulled out everything until I found my wallet. I opened it in such a hurry to see that I only had 27 cents left in my wallet. I forgot that I used the last few dollars on gas. Coming to this realization, I knew that I needed to make a hasty decision now rather than later. Anything to provide for my child.

I got up from the floor and grabbed my keys and phone. I hollered out to Bash that I would be right back and to keep an ear out for anything. I left the apartment, hopped in my car, and drove back to the church. I could feel my stomach sink into my body. My grandparents are probably rolling around in their graves. My parents are smiling up at me from hell. God is probably sitting back on his throne watching me make my morally wrong choice. If there was ever a time for divine intervention, let it be now. I suppose the term, 'now' in God's book is defined as whenever

He decides to send help. We all have to suffer the consequences of our actions. For that, I must ask the Lord above to forgive me for I was about to sin once more. I pulled up in front of the Blessed MacKillop Church. There was another vehicle parked outside besides mine. Father Townsend must be inside. I parked my jalopy, jumped out of it, and ran up the steps into the body of the church.

"Father Townsend! Father Townsend! Hey, Father Townsend!" I screamed throughout the empty sanctuary. I imagined the deceased souls praying in the pews glaring at me. I did not care for them right now. All I needed to see was Father Townsend.

"Father Townsend!" I hollered again.

"Here, my child." a priest came rushing down the center aisle to meet me.

"Where's the fire, my dear?" he asked me. "In hell, which is where I'm headed. I need to make a confession, Father."

"Yes, my child. Right this way." Father Townsend took my hand and led me to the confessional booth. I went to one side and he went to the other. I did the sign of the cross and began to open my heart.

"Bless me, Father, for I have sinned. My last confession was…well…years ago. I have lied, cheated, stole, ran with the wrong crowd, and now, going back to the past to make ends meet." I took a deep breath to regain myself. "I am sorry for these and all of my sins." There was silence on the other end for a moment. Then, Father Townsend spoke up to me.

"Lennie, I have known you since you were Bash's age. I know your heart as God knows your heart. You have a beautiful soul and a bright spirit. You have always been a hardworking woman and I respect you for that. Your choices, however, I keep close to God about you. I pray and ask that He would lead you to righteousness. God can still get you there in these difficult times and He will provide. Always have faith, Lennie. It will help you in these dangerous waters. Say a Hail Mary on your way out of the church. Let the heavens hear your call." Father Townsend spoke to me. I understood and thanked him. I recited the Act of Contrition, Father prayed for me, and I left the confessional. On my way back down the aisle, I began to pray the Hail Mary. Perhaps the

deceased souls prayed along with me out of pity.
Upon touching the church doors, I turned around to
see Father Townsend staring at me. We made eye
contact and he did the sign of the cross to me. I
translated that to him telling me, 'Good luck'. I gave a
half smile to Father and left the church. Only God
knows when I will come back to repent for the
multitude of sins that will be added to my list in the
coming moments.

Back in my car, I sat for a moment in silence.
The time had come when I would make the decision
that I knew I would regret. Fortunately, I knew that
making this decision would help me and my son. I
took the deepest breath I could take and whipped out
my phone. I knew that I needed to take this job more
than ever. Anything to provide for my child. Just then,

I searched for the contact that read, 'Pig'. I dialed the number and listened to the phone ring. After a few rings, someone on the other end picked up - it was Jonas. I rolled my eyes but I knew I needed to do this for Bash.

"Hello?"

"Hey, Jonas"

"Aye, baby! How have ya been? It's been a minute since I heard your pretty voice! What can I do for you, little lady?"

"I hate you but I hate myself more that I need to ask you this. Jonas…

"6 o'clock sharp."

"What?"

"I'm no asshat, Lennie. I always knew you would come crawling back to Daddy. Besides, who am I to reject one of my best workers?"

"You make me sick."

"You called and I provided."

"Ugh"

"No need to act all snotty, baby girl. I knew you needed me."

"I'm not doing this for you. I'm doing this for our son, Bash."

"Right. You're only coming back for the little squirt? What about me? I'm giving you your old job back and I get no thanks?"

"Thank you, Jonas," I rolled my eyes, "but if you start mistreating me again, I'll be gone for good." I heard him laugh on the other end.

"Sure, sweetheart. You said that the first time. 6 o'clock sharp - don't make me regret this."

"You never have, Jonas." I hung up and took a deep breath. The things a mother would do for her child. I put the phone down and drove off back to the apartment complex. When I returned, I did not immediately go to my apartment. I went next door to my neighbor's apartment. I knocked on her door and waited until she came to answer it. She opened the door wearing her pajamas and an apron.

"Oh, hey there, Lennie baby. How are ya?!" she exclaimed. Olivia Paine aka Momma Liv had been a resident of Applewood Complex for nearly 38 years. She was like a mother to me and a grandma to Bash.

"Hi Momma Liv, I need to come to grab some things from the closet," I said, kindly.
"Oh sure! Come right on in, honey bun!" she said and let me inside her apartment. Although our places were built the same, it sure didn't seem like that when I

entered. The inside of her apartment looked like a billionaire's beach house. Tapestries of gold hung from the walls and glitter complimented the floors. The strong smell of lemon pepper chicken filled the room.

"It smells so good in here, Momma Liv."

"Thank you, baby! I am making my famous lemon pepper chicken with some grilled string beans alongside some Hawaiian rolls. Woo child, I'm already big but this right here is going to add another fat roll on my back." She laughed loudly and I couldn't help but to laugh with her. Momma Liv always puts someone in a good mood. I went to the closet to gather some items for work tonight. I had a duffle bag already filled with some items from the night I quit. I just needed to grab some more things.

"Sugar bear, where are you heading to?" Momma Liv asked from the kitchen.

"Um…work, Momma Liv," I answered.

"Work?! Honey, you found a job! That's wonderful!!" she exclaimed. I emerged from the closet with my duffle bag and met her in the kitchen.

"Where are you working?" she asked.

"Back with Jonas" I responded, hesitantly.

"Back with Jonas?! Back with the sourpuss of a father?!"

"Yes, Momma Liv."

"If you needed some money, all you had to do was ask."

"I know, but I don't want to mooch off of you. This is just until I can balance out my finances." Momma Liv didn't look too pleased but she accepted my decision.

"Alright, you wanna take a plate to work tonight?" Momma Liv asked.

"No thanks, Momma Liv, I'll eat when I get to work," I said walking towards the door, "May Bash come over and have dinner with you?"

"Of course! Baby bear is always welcome over here! Are you sure you don't want a plate?" she asked with her hand on her hip.

"I'm fine, Momma Liv. I promise I'll eat when I get to work." Momma Liv walked over to me and gave me a tight hug.

"Be careful, Lennie. All money ain't good money," she said in my ear.

"I will, but I have to do what's best to keep food in my son's stomach."

"I understand," she said and released me from her grasp.

"I will tell Bash to head over here soon."

"That sounds perfect!" I bid Momma Liv goodbye and headed back to my raggedy, old shack.

Once inside my apartment, I looked at the clock stove. It was a little after 4:15 in the afternoon. I decided to head to the bathroom to take a shower, do my hair, and take care of other necessities. What seemed like an hour goes by and I am done getting dressed for work. I had on some gray sweatpants, a gray jacket, and some tennis shoes for the time being. My makeup was already completed before I left the bathroom. I looked at the time on my phone and it read 5:27 pm. I knocked on Bash's door and then proceeded to open it. Bash was still playing his game with friends over the internet. Bash looked up and saw me standing in the doorframe. He told his friends to hold on and he gave me his full attention.

"Hey Mom, what's up?"

"You're having dinner with Momma Liv tonight. So, put on your shoes and head over there to eat." I said. Bash nodded in agreement, said bye to his friends, and hopped off the game. He put on his house shoes and a hoodie over his Marvel shirt. Bash took notice of what I had on.

"Going somewhere?"

"Yeah. I-uh-got hired as a waitress and my first shift starts tonight."

"Mom, that's awesome! Another job serving delicious food." I forgot that was the lie I had told Bash originally. I wasn't ready to tell him that I was a stripper. A waitress at a 24-hour diner sounded more believable. Bash went to his backpack and pulled out a folded piece of paper.

"Here, Mom. I made this for you at school today." he handed me the paper.

"Thanks, Bash. I'll read it when I get to work." Bash hugged me and ran to the door. I yelled to him, "Make sure to say thank you. Momma Liv has a spare key to let you back in."

"I will. Do you want a plate?" he asked.

"No, I'll eat when I get to work. Just make sure you say thank you."

"Yes ma'am. Bye, Mom!" he said as he closed the door behind him. *Bye, baby bear* - I thought to myself. Those knots from earlier still stayed in my stomach. I just wasn't ready to tell Bash the truth yet. Guilt might as well be my dinner. As I grabbed my duffle bag from off the floor, I placed Bash's paper in there and then walked out the door. After a quick walk

from the door to the car, I opened the car door and

threw my bag on the passenger seat. I cut the engine

on and drove to work in silence. I wouldn't bother

listening to the radio tonight.

I arrived at my destination with time to spare. I

parked my car and cut off the engine. I took a few

deep breaths, grabbed my bag, and headed inside the

place. I went through the back door to avoid being

seen by Jonas for a few moments. Once inside, all of

the girls greeted me with open arms. I spoke to

everyone and then made my way to my locker.

"Nice to see you again, Lennie."

"Likewise, Whitley." Whitley was the one who taught

me how to be a stripper. Over the years, she became

the only person I could trust at this establishment.

"We've got ourselves a full house tonight. We're gonna walk away with lots of cash."

"I bet."

"Why the long face, Lennie? Something wrong?"

"No, Whitley. I'm just doing what a mother should do for her child - provide."

"Can't relate since I ain't got children. I only provide for me and my sweet ass." Whitley laughed. I smiled at Whitley while changing into tonight's outfit. Suddenly, a voice came from the entrance of the locker room. Everyone in the room hushed when it spoke.

"My favorite, welcome back." It was Jonas - that 5'11, big, burly, black-haired no-good demon walked over to me. He pushed past Whitley to stand directly in front of me.

"Jonas," I mumbled.

"Sweet, sugar lips decided to come back to Daddy. I knew you missed me." he grinned.

"You know, someone else wishes that they could meet their daddy."

"I told you my suggestions years ago - abortion or adoption. You ignored me."

"If you only knew what kind of young man he is, Jonas. Bash is gonna be a better man than you."

"Alright, I'll see him in a news article. Until then, you go shake that pretty ass and bring in some bank." Jonas said, patting my shoulders before walking off.

"Alright, everybody! Time to make me rich as hell!" he yelled and the girls filed out of the locker room. I was still putting on the remainder of my clothes. I reached back into my duffle bag for my iridescent heels. My hand brushed over the paper

Bash had given me. I pulled it out, sat on the bench, and read it. I opened the folded paper to see two stick figures drawn on top of the Earth. There were yellow stars drawn around the planet and what looked like a shooting star floating off into the distance. Below the earth, Bash had written a note to me. The note said,

"I am so happy that you're my mom and are always there for me. The world would be a happier place if there were more people like you. Love you! - Bash." Tears began to form in my eyes. My motivation, my love, my Sebastian. I wiped my eyes with my hand and put the note back in the bag. I pulled out my heels to put them on.

"Time is money, Lennie," Jonas said from the doorframe. I was so caught up in Bash's illustration that I didn't notice Jonas.

"I'm coming. Chill." I said while fastening the straps on my heels. Jonas just stood there and smiled at me. Once I finished, I stood up and walked towards the door. Jonas stretched his arm out to block me from leaving. He leaned into my ear and I felt his haunting breath hit my skin.

"I've missed you."
"I've got work to do," I said and pushed his arm down. Jonas smiled showing his snow-white teeth. I walked out the door and onto the stage - showtime.

The night was wild and full of dark magic. Divorced daddies and rich, working men all came in that night and drained their pockets. It was 3:00 in the morning and the club was closed. The girls each collected the remaining bills from the stage and brought them to the locker room. The rule was if you grab it first, then the money is yours. I sat down on the bench and counted my winnings. I ended up making $550 that night. Although my guilt was still present, I felt relieved that I could provide for Bash. I put my money in the duffle bag along with my heels. One by one, the girls changed their clothes, packed their things, and left the club. About 12 minutes later, it was only me, Whitley, and two other girls. I was finishing putting my tennis shoes back on when Whitley came over to me.

"You did good tonight. Proud of you," she said, placing a comforting hand on my shoulder. "Thanks," I responded.

"Get home safe and I'll see you tomorrow?" "I'll see you tomorrow." We smiled at each other and Whitley left. I looked around my space to make sure I had everything I brought with me. I grabbed my bags, said goodbye to the remaining two girls, and left the club. When I got to my car, I heard a voice call me from behind.

"Lennie, wait up!" Once again, it was Jonas. He did a little jog to catch up with me. As fit as he was, I could hear Jonas catching his breath - big wuss.

"Let me go home, Jonas."

"I will, but I just wanna say…you haven't lost your touch."

"Thanks"

"You know, I can give you an immediate raise right now. You can work as a private entertainer. You and the clients can have a one-on-one experience. What do you say? You in?"

"Being a private entertainer is the reason Bash is here now or don't you remember."

"Lennie…"

"I am grateful that I get to provide for OUR son. Even if it takes coming back to old habits. As long as Bash is healthy and happy, I am happy." There was silence for a moment as Jonas and I stared at each other. Jonas stepped forward and tried to place his hands around my waist. I backed up and opened my car door. I threw my bag in and hopped in the driver's seat. Jonas held the car door open with his hand. I pulled out my keys and started the engine. I directed my attention back to Jonas.

"Let it go."

"Fine. I better see you tomorrow," he said smiling.

He let go of the door and closed it. Jonas remained standing there smiling as I pulled out of the club's parking spot. His standing there reminded me of the statues from the church - judging despite appearance. I drove off back to my small apartment. Before I got home, I stopped by an open convenience store. I went inside to grab some milk, 2 small Frosted Flakes boxes, 2 bananas, and 2 granola bars. I figured I might as well get something for breakfast, and then go grocery shopping later in the day. I paid for the items, hopped back in the car, and drove off to home. I ate one of the bananas while driving.

Surprisingly, the same parking spot from earlier was still vacant when I arrived. I pulled in and cut off the engine. I grabbed only the convenience store bag and left my duffle bag in the car. Out of the car and up the steps to my door. I unlocked my front door and walked inside to see the light from Bash's room was on. I went to the kitchen to put up the "groceries" and threw away my banana peel in the trash. Once all was put up, I started to walk towards Bash's room. Something caught my eye while I passed the couch. I saw a sleeping figure on the couch wrapped in a blanket. Bash was asleep on the couch. I walked over to him and sat down on the floor right by his head. I pulled back the blanket so I could kiss him on his cheek. After I gave him a smooch, I lay down on the floor and fell asleep. At that moment, I made a vow that we would never experience another rabbit food weekend.

PART / TWO

I woke up the next morning forgetting that I

had fallen asleep on the floor. Once I was fully awake,

I realized that there was something on top of me -

something comfy. It was a blanket. Not just any

blanket - the one Bash was using last night. I sat up on

the floor and stretched. I've noticed that you hear

more noises from your body as you get older. There

were several pops and bops but I embraced anyway. I

looked over to the couch and did not see my son. So, I

got off the floor still wearing my jacket and

sweatpants. When I stood up, I looked around for my

phone. I thought I had it with me but I must've left it

in the car. Then, a voice spoke to me from the

hallway.

"Morning, Mom." I turned my head towards the direction of the sound and saw my son looking at me.

"Good morning, sunshine," I said tiredly, "how are you?"

"Good. How was your night?" he asked.

"It was…good. Tiring but good."

"That's good." Bash smiled at me. I smiled back at him. The light from the window caught my eye, so I turned to look at the clock on the stove. The clock read 9:34 in the morning.

"Ah! You're late! Bash, hurry, and take a shower. I gotta get you to school." I yelled.

"Mom. Mom!"

"What?!"

"Mom, chill. It's Saturday. I don't have school today."

I froze in my tracks.

"What do you mean?"

"Mom, yesterday was Friday and today is Saturday.

There's no school today." I couldn't believe it. I had

lost my mind for sure.

"Mom, are you okay?" Bash walked up to me

and looked me dead in my eyes. I had to lie.

"Yes. I'm fine." I pulled him for a hug and

kissed the top of his head.

My heart ached for him. He had to live with a

mother who was worthless and never knew that his

father was a slimy worm. I had become my mother.

She was once an entertainer herself and daddy was a

businessman. Let's just say that Daddy reaped what

he sowed and lost what he sold. Now, both of my

parents rot beneath my feet. I just kept hugging my son for dear life. I wanted to be better than my parents. I wanted to provide for my child the right way. I'm still trying to find the right way. I pulled back and looked into my son's eyes. I teared up myself. In his eyes, I saw faith and hope restored for both of us.

"Mom?"

"Yes, baby?"

"Why are you crying?"

"Because," I choked, "because I love you so much and I move the planets and stars for you."

"You can do that?"

"I can do anything." We laughed and embraced once more.

"I love you, Mom."

"I love you too, stink." We pulled away and Bash went back into his room. I remained where I was for a moment reminiscing on the memories Bash and I had made over the years. It had only been us this entire time. No Jonas. No parents. My grandparents died when I was in high school. I had no connection to any other family except Bash.

I decided to take a shower to wash the funk of last night off of me. I went to the bathroom, took off last night's clothes, and turned the shower on. As the shower water was running, I stood in front of the bathroom mirror. Just stared at myself. I barely recognized the person that I had become. A single mother of one working at a night joint just to make ends meet. Would God forgive me for this mess? I don't know. Suddenly, I heard a scream so loud that it could shatter a stained glass window. I hurriedly shut off the water, jumped out of the shower, and wrapped myself in a towel. Just when I was letting the water soothe my skin, something always happens - I blame the author.

I flung open the window with one hand while the other was holding my towel. Water is dripping down on the ground from my hair and body. I ran into the living room to find that the front door was open and Bash was standing on the threshold. I could hear that there was some sort of commotion going on outside that had Bash mesmerized.

"Bash," I said. He jumped at the sound of my voice and turned to me.

"Yes, Mom." his innocent voice asked.

"The heck is going on? Who screamed?"

"Momma Liv is out here yelling and beating a man with a baseball bat."

"What does the bat look like?"

"Ummm…metal. It looks like a metal bat."

"Sweet Jesus." When Momma Liv grabbed her bat, it was something serious and I had to help her. I walked past Bash to step out to see what was the problem. No shoes - just a wrapped towel around my drenched figure. I stepped out and looked to my left. Momma Liv was holding the bat above her as she yelled at the man. I walked over to her to see if I could help.

"Get up! Get up, devil! Let me show ya what I'm made of." she yelled. The man was lying on the ground in a fetal position.

"Momma Liv, what's going on?"

"You tell me," she said, aiming the bat at the man on the ground.

"What are you talking about?" Upon my asking that question, the man on the ground moved to where I could see his face. The man was Jonas.

"Jonas" I whispered. I could not believe that he was here. Without thinking, I grabbed the bat from Momma Liv with my free hand and prepared to swing it at Jonas's stomach. He was already down, so I had a chance to finish him off.

"Lennie! Lennie! Lennie! Wait! Please, wait!" he begged.
"Shut up!"

"Lennie, please! Let me explain!" Jonas could barely get out those words through his groans of pain.

"What?! Why are you here?!"
"I came to see you."

"See you?!", Momma Liv jumped in, "Lennie, this is happening again?!" she said pointing back and forth between me and Jonas.

"No, Momma Liv. *This* is done and dead."

"So what is he talking about?" I directed my attention back to Jonas.

"Explain yourself, Jonas."

"May I get up?"

"No!" Momma Liv and I both yelled at him.

"Fine. I came see to you so I could give you something"

"What, herpes?"

"Momma Liv"

"Hey - he looks like the type."

"No, not herpes. I don't even have herpes."

"Sure, nitwit." Momma Liv said under her breath.

"I - I came by to give you your phone," Jonas said. He slowly reached into his pocket and pulled out my phone. I handed the bat back to Momma Liv and took my phone from him. Momma Liv kept the bat pointing directly at him just in case he made any sudden moves.

"Thanks," I said.

"Sure. Now, can I get up?" Momma Liv and I exchanged looks.

"Slowly." Momma Liv told him. Jonas gradually got his aching body off of the ground. I knew he would be pretty bruised up the way he groaned. Once he stood tall, he made eye contact with me. Then, he shifted his eyes over to Momma Liv who was still aiming the bat at him.

"You can lower the bat now."

"Make me." Momma Liv stood firm on her words.

Jonas rolled his eyes and looked back at me.

"Leave, Jonas," I said.

"Okay. I'll leave. Just make sure you're on time

tonight. Lots of people come out to party on Saturday

night."

"Fine. I'll be there."

"Can I come?" a voice came from my right. All eyes

looked over at Bash. He was standing outside the door

of our apartment.

"Bash, honey. H - How long have you been

standing there?" I asked my child.

"I never went back inside. I wanted to see what was

going on and wanted to make sure that you guys were

okay."

"We're fine, baby." Momma Liv said to him.

"Yeah, we're fine. Just a little misunderstanding." I
added after her. I noticed how Bash's eyes moved
from me over to a frozen Jonas. The two brown-eyed
boys pondered at the sight of each other for a
moment. I moved closer to my son and knelt at his
height. I took a deep breath and glanced over to
Momma Liv. She nodded her head at me as she knew
what I was about to do.

"Bash," I started, "I want you to meet
someone. This man right here is…"
"Dad," Bash said. The air in my lungs clenched itself
at the sound of his words.
"Y-yes. How did you know that?"
"When Father Townsend would pray for me, he would
pray for my dad and then, one day I asked him if he
knew anything of my dad. He fits the description

Father Townsend gave me" Bash said, pointing at Jonas. I looked at Jonas who had fear in his eyes and feelings hidden from his heart. Momma Liv lowered the bat from Jonas's body. My son walked over to meet his father. Bash stuck out his hand for Jonas to shake.

"Hi. I'm Sebastian but I go by Bash." Jonas slowly shook Bash's hand.
"Nice to meet you, young man."

"Nice to meet you, too. I've always wanted to meet you." Jonas gave a nervous half-smile.

"Where have you been? I have so much to tell you. About the school, about my friends, and oh! I made this cool sculpture in art class the other day. You wanna see it?"
"Uh. Sure, kid."

"Awesome! Hang tight - I need to go find it. I'll be right back." Bash turned to run inside the apartment. First, he turned back to Jonas and hugged him. Bash is so short that he can only hug Jonas's waist. This action caught everyone by surprise. Bash let go and ran inside of the apartment. Jonas stood there with racing thoughts and emotions. I could tell by his body language. Jonas and I made eye contact and I couldn't help but smile at him. The moment I had been dreaming of had come true. Sadly, the dream would not turn out to be what I wanted. Jonas did a quick 180 and started walking back to his car.

"Hey!" I called out to him. I followed behind him barefoot and all. I asked Momma Liv to keep an eye out for Bash. Before Jonas could make it to his car, I chucked my phone at the back of his head. It hit him hard and stopped him right in his tracks. He quickly turned around and faced me.

"What?!"

"You're just gonna leave like that?! Really, Jonas?!"

"Look! I told you years ago to get rid of that kid. I didn't ask for this! I never signed up to be a parent."

"Neither did I but whose fault is that?!"

"Yours!"

"Mine!"

"Yes! I thought you wanted a special night with me but no, you wanted more than a special night. You wanted to be a mother!"

"How dare you?! That was not what I was going for and you know that! You and I shared one too many drinks that night and things went too far! Look at what our lives have become! Why can't you accept

that we are parents now, Jonas!"

"Because we are not meant to be parents! We

were meant to make money together and swim in it!

We were supposed to live like royalty and indulge in

life's delicious wonders! He was never a part of the

plan!"

"He is now and you'll have to deal with it!"

"I don't want him and neither should you!"

"I want him! I love him! I'm keeping him!" At

this point, I had tears streaming down my enraged

face.

"You're crazy. You know what? Forget it. I'll see you

later on tonight."

"No."

"No?"

"No. I quit. I'm not going back." Jonas gave a little snicker.

"Lennie, be for real right now. You need me."

"I don't need you, Jonas."

"You need me!"

"I don't need you! All I needed was to find a way to make sure that our child had food in his belly! The tips from last night helped me and yes, I had planned on staying there for some time but after what you just displayed in front of me…I quit."

"Lennie, Lennie, Lennie. You're making a mistake."

"The mistake I made was ever doing business with the likes of you."

"Fine. Fine! If that's what you want then that is your decision. Hope you can find a way to provide for that little boy of yours."

"Oh, I will. I'm taking you to court so you can start paying child support."

"Girl, please. You don't have any money."

"God will provide for me!"

"Oh, he will?"

"Yes, he will!"

"Well, if he is going to provide for you then why hasn't provided for you now? Hmm? Where has he been?"

"Stop it, Jonas!"

"No! You stop it, Lennie! When will you wake up from this silly ass dream?! You made this bed so now you gotta lay in it!"

"Jonas"

"No! If you want to go to war, then let's go to war. You literally have nothing to lose." And with that, Jonas walked away from me and got in his car. He turned on the engine and sped off from the apartment complex. I stood there with tears down my face and my head hung low in defeat. I did make this bed so now I must lay in it.

I took my available hand and wiped my face of the wet anger that fell from my eyes. As I turned around, I noticed two figures at the top of the staircase. It was Bash and Momma Liv. Momma Liv looked distraught while Bash looked upset as he held his sculpture in his hands. The silence between us was loud. I didn't know what to do at that moment. How much did he see? I took a step forward back towards the stairs. When I did that, Bash took a step back. I took another step forward and Bash took another step back. My heart sank inside of my chest. I choked on my tears. One more step forward and Bash took one more step back.

"Bash…" I softly called out to him. Bash shook his head at me - disgusted.

"Bash…" I called for him again. He took off back inside the apartment. I ran from where I stood back up the stairs. Before I ran back inside of my hole, I stopped in front of Momma Liv.

"Momma Liv, I thought I told you to watch him."

"I did, baby love, but…he really wanted to show Jonas what he made. I'm sorry."

"It's okay," I told her. Before I could walk past her, Momma Liv held out some clothes in front of me.

"I grabbed a shirt and some pants for you. I figured you'd get tired of holding that towel around you." I smiled at her. I dropped the towel from around me and let it meet the ground. I did not care who or what may see my body. We are all of the same kind. I threw the shirt and pants that Momma Liv had got for me. I went to reach for the towel but Momma Liv stopped me.

"Go see your child." I nodded my head at her and dashed inside the apartment. Dirty feet and all, I walked down the hall and stood outside of Bash's room. There I stood - afraid. Fearing what he would say, his anger towards me, and not having the answers to some of his questions. I took a deep, deep breath before knocking on the door.

"Bash, honey, may I come in?" I asked

through the door. No response.

"Bash". There still wasn't a response. I cracked open

the door a little and could not see him. Then, I opened

the door entirely and scanned the room for my son.

There was no sight of him. I stepped inside to take

note of his room. A tidy bed, toys put away, clear

floor, and his…his sculpture in the trash. I walked

over to the trash can and picked up the piece of art.

The sculpture was a man made out of clay holding

what appeared to be a spear. Maybe the person was a

caveman; how clever. I placed the sculpture on his

desk. I looked around the room once more to see

where Bash could have been. Then, my attention was

directed towards the closet. The closet door was

barely opened. My intuition convinced me to check

inside. I walked over to the closet and opened the

door. Sure enough, I found my baby boy sitting on the floor with his arms crossed and knees to chest. I got down on the ground to be his equal. There was a loud moment of silence. No one said anything to the other. We simply just sat there. Soon, I spoke up to my son.

"Bash," I started, "I'm sorry you had to see that scene. You shouldn't have witnessed that monstrosity."

"He wants nothing to do with me."

"Bash, he - "

"He wants nothing to do with me. I heard him." I sighed. "Is that why you don't talk about him?"

"Something like that."

"Mom"

"Yes, baby?"

"Can you be honest with me?"

"Of course. What would you like to know?"

"If he wants nothing to do with me, why did you go back to him?" I paused for a moment. I knew I had to tell him the truth but the truth hurts worse than being cut. I thought about how to carefully answer my son.

"I went back to him because I knew I had to do something to provide for you; for us. We were running low on money and I knew that working one shift with Jonas would help us out big time. Yes, it was a wrong decision but I did it for you; for us."

"You told him that you believe that God would provide for us? Did you lie?"

"I didn't lie. I-I merely said what was on my heart. My mind overruled my heart and decided to do things its own way."

"Oh."

"I remember Father Townsend spoke about how God will get us to where we are meant to be and give us all that we desire. The path isn't straightforward from point A to point B. Our fated path requires us to run a few errands before arriving at our dream come true. I keep trying to understand that but I am human. I was born to be bruised."

"Do you think we are almost there?"

"At our dream come true?"

"Yes"

"I don't know. What I do know is that we will get there soon. I promise." Bash smiled at me. I back at him. He had his father's eyes and smile. It made my nerves shake with anger to be reminded of someone so wicked. Yet, I know deep in my heart that Bash will never be anything like Jonas.

"I wouldn't want to work for him. Can't you find another waitress job somewhere where he's not?"

"Maybe I'll look into other places outside of waiting tables."

"Okay. I just want you to also take care of yourself. I need you, Mom." Tears began to form in my eyes. I pulled Bash in closer to me and kissed the top of his head. I held him close to me fearing that I would blink and he wouldn't be there. Bash pulled away from me and looked into my eyes.

"So, what happens now, Mom?" I took a deep breath.

"Now, we prepare for battle. War is coming."